Christmas Party™

by Ellen Reymes

DUALSTAR PUBLICATIONS   PARACHUTE PRESS

SCHOLASTIC INC.
New York Toronto London Auckland Sydney

DUALSTAR PUBLICATIONS  PARACHUTE PRESS

Dualstar Publications
c/o 10100 Santa Monica Blvd.
Suite 2200
Los Angeles, CA 90067

Parachute Press
156 Fifth Avenue
Suite 325
New York, NY 10010

Published by Scholastic Inc.

With special thanks to Robert Thorne, Harold Weitzberg, and Vail Associates.

Printed in the U.S.A.
October 1997
ISBN: 0-590-76958-8
A B C D E F G H I J

"This is going to be our best Christmas party ever!" Ashley exclaimed.

I stared at her in disbelief. "Did you forget our party last year in Vail, Colorado?" I asked. "*That* was the best Christmas party ever!"

I'm Mary-Kate Olsen. My sister Ashley and I are twins. We're both nine years old. We both have big blue eyes and strawberry blond hair.

We look alike, but we don't think alike.

Especially when it comes to Christmas parties!

"Why do you think last year's party was better?" Ashley asked.

"Simple," I replied. "Because last year's party had plenty of snow! Don't you remember?"

"How could I forget!" Ashley exclaimed.

It all began when we called our friends Allie, Clarissa, Kelly, and Sarah to invite them to our party.

"Please say you can come," I told them over the phone.

"We definitely can!" Clarissa declared. Allie and Kelly agreed.

"Me too," Sarah said. "Though it's too bad there isn't any snow around here. You know I love sledding and skiing. Why, I'm a great skier!"

"Then you'll love our party," I said. "Because it will be in the mountains, in Vail, Colorado. We'll have *plenty* of snow!"

"You could even teach us how to ski," Ashley said.

"Uh—sure—" Sarah began.

"There's no time to talk about it now," I said. "Let's all meet at the airport in one hour."

Ashley let out a cheer. "Colorado, here we come!"

We stepped off the plane. Deep white snow covered the ground. It glistened on the treetops. It sparkled on the rooftops.

Everywhere around us people zipped down the sides of Snow Mountain on skis and sleds.

"Sarah, you have to teach us how to ski right now!" I exclaimed.

"Um, I'm not ready to ski yet," Sarah said. "Let's play laser tag!"

We love playing laser tag. We bring laser blasters wherever we go. We handed them out to all of our friends and a few other kids.

WHIZZZ! ZINGGG! ZAAP!

I blasted Ashley.

Ashley zapped me back. "I got you! You're out!" she exclaimed.

I fell onto my knees, laughing. Everyone turned around and zapped Ashley back!

"That was fun," I said when the game was over. "But can we ski now?"

"Let's find our cabin first," Sarah said. "I can't wait to hang our stockings."

"Good idea!" Clarissa grinned. "Then Santa—" Her eyes suddenly opened wide with horror. "Oh, no! This is terrible! Our Christmas is totally ruined!"

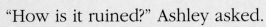

"How is it ruined?" Ashley asked.

"We're so far from home!" Clarissa replied. "How will Santa know where to bring our presents?"

"You're right! This is terrible!" Ashley exclaimed. "Mary-Kate and I wanted ice skates for Christmas. We'll never get them now!"

Kelly laughed. "Don't be silly! Santa will find us wherever we are."

"No, he won't!" Allie declared. Now she looked unhappy, too.

"Don't worry," I said. "We'll put a Christmas tree in the window of our cabin. We'll hang our names on the tree. Santa will see them, and he'll know we're here."

"Plus, the tree will look nice for our party!" Sarah added.

"Good thinking," Ashley declared. "Let's go buy our tree right now!"

We raced down the path toward town.

"Ooooomph!"

Allie knocked into Ashley. Ashley fell right into the snow.

"Hey!" she exclaimed in surprise.

"Sorry! I didn't mean to knock you down," Allie said. "I thought I saw a bear in that tree." She pointed to a nearby pine tree.

I stared at the tree. There was no bear there now.

"Hey! Look at me!" Ashley shouted. "Watch this!"

Ashley swept her arms and legs back and forth in the snow.

She was making a...

...snow angel!

"Cool! I want to make one, too!" I said.

"You can't—we still need our tree," Clarissa reminded us.

"You're right. And there's the perfect place to buy it." I pointed across the mountain to Vail Village.

"It's a very long walk from here to there," Sarah said.

"Maybe we won't have to walk," I replied.

"Then how will we get there?" Kelly asked.

"Simple!" I grinned. "We'll take a...

"…snow tube!"

Our friends jumped into colorful tubes and zoomed down the hill.

Ashley and I jumped into tubes of our own and sped after them.

It was so much fun! We laughed all the way.

"Hey, did anybody see that bear in his tube?" Allie asked when we reached the bottom of the hill.

"Bear? What bear?" I looked around. I didn't see a bear anywhere.

"Don't be silly," Sarah said. "There are no bears on this mountain."

"And bears don't know how to snow tube!" Clarissa laughed.

"But I'm sure I saw a bear," Allie said.

"You couldn't have," Kelly told her.

We left our tubes by the covered bridge and hurried into Vail Village. Along the way, Allie kept looking for her bear.

The village was crowded with people. Ashley and I led the way to the place where they sold Christmas trees. The others soon followed.

"Ho, ho, hello!" a deep voice boomed. "My name is Nick!"

I gasped and rubbed my eyes.

"Ashley," I whispered. "Do you see what I see?"

Up ahead we saw a tree salesman. He wore a bright red parka.

He had a long, curly white beard. And a big round belly.

"I see him," Ashley replied. "And he looks just like Santa!"

We all ran toward the tree salesman. Sarah led the way. Then came Ashley and me, Kelly, Clarissa, and Allie.

"Ho, ho, how can I help you?" Nick asked.

"We want one special, perfect Christmas tree for our party, please," I replied.

Ashley pointed to a nearby tree hung with bright decorations. "A tree just like that one," she said.

"I have only one tree left." Nick held up a skinny, scraggly little pine tree.

"Oh, no!" Clarissa cried. "That tree won't work!"

"It has to be perfect for Santa," Sarah explained.

"Santa won't mind if your tree isn't perfect," Nick said. "All that's really important is to have Christmas spirit."

He smiled. "But why don't you try the other Christmas tree lot. It's back across the mountain. Just remember one important thing!"

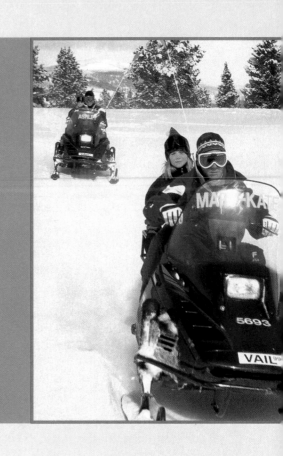

"What's that?" I asked.

"The lot closes at four o'clock sharp," Nick said. "So don't be late!"

"No problem! We'll just take a taxi," Clarissa said.

"What taxi?" Allie laughed. "There are no taxis here. There aren't even any roads."

Ashley snapped her fingers. "But I know another way we can ride across the mountain!"

"How?" I asked.

"On snowmobiles!" Ashley cried. "Let's go!"

We hurried to Big Bob's Snowmobile Palace. We each jumped into a snowmobile with a grown-up driver.

"To the other side of the mountain, please," I shouted.

We zipped over the mountain top.
We plowed through fields of snow.
We zoomed from one side of Snow Mountain to
the other.
It was great!

I checked my watch. We still had time to learn
to ski before we picked up our Christmas tree!
But Ashley had a totally different idea.
She wanted to...

...build a snowman!

And that's exactly what we did!

We carved out a *giant* snowman! He had a big, wide bottom. A medium-sized stomach. And a huge, moon-shaped head.

We added small dark stones for two eyes and a nose.

Then we added a row of stones for a curving, smiling mouth.

Last of all, we placed evergreen branches on his head for fluffy green hair.

We looked at him—and burst out laughing. Our snowman looked so silly!

"That was fun. But now we *have* to ski," I said.

"Not yet!" Sarah pulled out her laser blaster. "First, let's play another game of laser tag!"

"No more tag," Allie said. "I'm going skiing!" She started to run toward the ski slopes.

"Be careful!" Ashley called after her. "There's ice on the ground. Try not to slip!"

But Allie was staring up at the ski slope. She didn't see the ice on the ground.

"Allie!" Ashley yelled. "Look out!"

Too late!

Allie slipped on the ice. She crashed into Sarah. *SPLAT!*

Sarah went flying. She landed in a snow bank.

"I'm so sorry!" Allie cried. "I didn't see you! I was looking at that skiing bear!"

"What skiing bear?" Sarah asked. We all turned to look at the ski slope.

"I don't see any bear," Clarissa said.

"And bears don't know how to ski!" Kelly added.

"There *was* a bear! I saw him!" Allie exclaimed. "You didn't look fast enough, or you would have seen him, too!"

"Forget about the bear," I declared. "It's time to ski!"

We all put on our skis and grabbed ski poles. Ashley and I were ready first. Allie and Sarah fastened their skis next.

"Sarah, start our lesson!" I called over my shoulder.

Sarah suddenly grabbed her leg. "Ow! My ankle!" she moaned. "I think I sprained it! You guys will have to go skiing without me!"

"Well, okay," I said. We slowly moved away.

We all felt bad for Sarah. But we were also excited about learning to ski.

And we didn't know that we were in for a big surprise. Everyone was getting ready for a ski race!

"Hurry!" the ski instructor told us. "You need a team number to ski in the race."

"We can't be in a race," I said. "We don't know how to ski very well yet."

"You have just enough time to learn more." The instructor showed us everything we needed to know. And we learned really fast!

We raced to the chair lift and checked it out.
Allie stared at the top of the mountain. She gasped. "The bear!" she exclaimed. "He's riding the chair lift!"

"Where?" Ashley asked. We all gazed up to look for the bear.

"There's no bear on this lift," Clarissa said.

"You missed him again!" Allie groaned. "He's gone now!"

Hmmmmmm.

Was Allie seeing things? I wondered.

It was our turn to climb onto the chair lift.

We rode up to the mountain top. Then we hurried to the starting shed. That's where the race would begin.

"Attention, everyone!" the race announcer called. "Get ready...set...

…ski!"
The race was on!

"Yahoo!"

We flew down the mountain.

We knew we weren't good enough to win the race—but we sure had fun!

We swooped down to the finish line. Everyone there cheered!

Ashley and I slapped our first high-five—on skis!

"Hooray! You guys were fantastic!" a familiar voice called.

Sarah?

We spotted her standing off by herself. And she was jumping up and down, waving her arms in the air!

"You were incredible!" Sarah exclaimed. "How did you learn to ski so fast?" she asked.

"How did your ankle get better so fast?" I asked.

"Ooops!" Sarah's face turned bright red.

"Your ankle isn't hurt! You lied to us!" Allie exclaimed.

"How could you!" Clarissa exploded.

"Why did you?" Kelly demanded.

Sarah burst into tears!

Ashley and I felt confused as we waited for Sarah to explain.

"I'm sorry," Sarah finally said. "I didn't mean to lie. But I'm a terrible skier! I couldn't teach anyone how to ski."

"Why didn't you just say so?" I asked.

"I was too embarrassed." Sarah sniffled. "I was afraid you'd make fun of me."

"We would never do that," Ashley told her.

"Of course not," Clarissa chimed in. "You don't need to be great at everything to be a great friend."

Sarah blinked in surprise. "Do you really mean that?"

"Really," I said with a grin. We all gave Sarah a big hug.

"I feel so much better," Sarah said.

"But I don't!" Clarissa exclaimed. "It's five minutes to four—and we *still* don't have our Christmas tree! Let's go!"

We quickly taught Sarah everything we learned about skiing. Then we all skied to the other Christmas tree lot. It sat near the top of a hill.

"Ho, ho, hello again!" Nick called.

"Nick! What are you doing *here*?" I asked.

Nick chuckled. "I own *both* tree lots. That's how I was able to save the right tree for you! Hope it makes you ho, ho, happy!"

Nick showed us the most beautiful Christmas tree ever!

"But now I have to dash," he said. "I'm a very busy man!" He hopped onto a snowmobile and zoomed away.

I grinned at Ashley. Ashley grinned at me. "This tree is perfect!" I said in delight.

"But how will we get it down the hill?" Sarah asked.

We were trying to figure it out when something rustled in the treetops overhead.

"It's the bear!" Allie shrieked. She jumped back in alarm—and bumped right into our Christmas tree.

The tree wiggled. It wobbled. Then it toppled over—and went flying down the hill!

By the time we caught our tree, it wasn't beautiful anymore.

"I'm sorry!" Allie groaned. "I thought I saw that bear again. Now I ruined our tree—and our party!"

"No, you haven't," Ashley told her. "Remember what Nick said. All Santa cares about is having Christmas spirit. And we've got plenty of that!"

"So let's start the party!" I said.

We had our Christmas party—and it was fantastic!

Best of all, Allie never mentioned that bear again.

Before we went to bed that night, I set out a glass of milk and a plateful of cookies for Santa.

VRRROOOMMM!! VRRROOOMMM!!

We woke up with a start. "What was that scary noise?" Ashley asked.

We hugged each other tight.

"Let's go check it out!" I exclaimed.

We hurried to the window. We saw Nick on his snowmobile roaring away from the cabin.

"It was just Nick," I said. "But why are Santa's milk and cookies all gone?"

"And why is there a heap of presents under the tree?" Ashley added. "Including the brand-new ice skates we wanted so much?"

I frowned. "Do you think Nick really *is* Santa?" *Hmmmmm.*

41

"We never did figure out last year if Nick was Santa, did we?" Ashley asked.

"No, we didn't," I replied. "And we never saw Allie's bear, either."

Brriiiing!

The doorbell rang. Our friends had arrived. It was time to start this year's Christmas party!

We greeted everyone and the fun began!

"You know, Ashley," I said. "Thinking about last year's party reminded me of something very important. We should always remember to keep the true spirit of Christmas."

"You mean the spirit of giving, and sharing, and friendship?" Ashley asked.

"That's right. Because it doesn't matter if you have a perfect tree—" I began.

"Or the fanciest decorations, or a mountain full of white, glittering snow," Ashley finished.

"Right!" I smiled. "Those things don't matter at all. What really matters is—"

"Sharing Christmas with your very best friends!" I exclaimed.

"And giving them something really special!" Ashley added. She held out three beautiful, silvery snowflake necklaces. She handed one to each of our friends.

"Wow!" they cried. "Thanks, Mary-Kate and Ashley!" All our friends gave us each a hug.

"You're welcome," I told them. "And Ashley and I thank *you*—because as long as we're together, *every* Christmas will be the very best Christmas ever!"

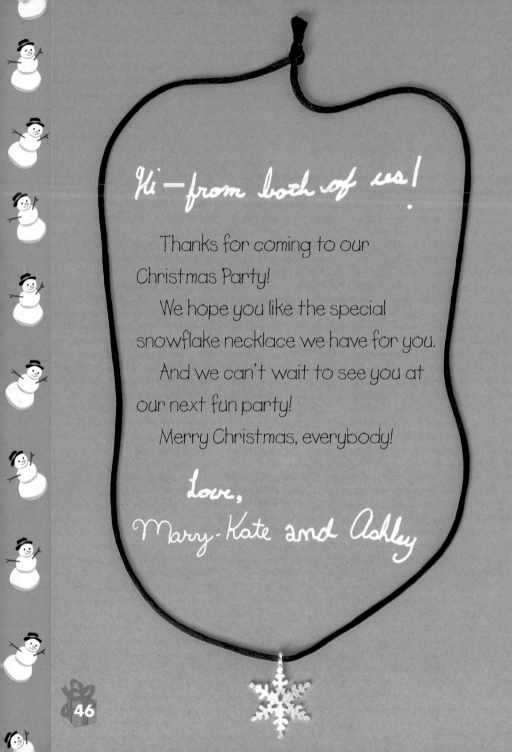

Hi — from both of us!

Thanks for coming to our
Christmas Party!
We hope you like the special
snowflake necklace we have for you.
And we can't wait to see you at
our next fun party!
Merry Christmas, everybody!

Love,
Mary-Kate and Ashley